LATTJO

Perfect Party

LATTJO

Perfect Party

Down in the Underworld, Rosa, the Root Queen, gathered her friends together. It was so much fun to be around Mu, the young mummy, Viktor, the vampire, the silly ghosts, and her over-protective bats. She knew they'd make a wonderful addition to any celebration.

"I have an announcement everybody!" she said. "There's going to be a special 'Last Day of Summer' party in the Garden today. And it's only right for us to share in the fun!"

"They would never expect to see us in the Garden," Mu said.

"I'm hungry already," added Viktor.

"Ready, set, go!" the ghosts shouted out one at a time, tripping over each other.

The Root Queen's Bat Squad zoomed off for the Garden to check things out.

4

Meanwhile, everyone from the Funhouse and Garden scurried around preparing for their celebration. There was to be fun and games and lots of cake!

"Is everything ready?" asked the Royal Queen.

"All but the cake," answered the Wizard.

"Then bake away!" the Royal Queen proclaimed.

Hidden in the bushes, the Bat Squad watched. It was their job to make sure everything was safe for the Root Queen's visit.

One of the bats got his wings tangled up with a balloon. He accidentally poked a hole in it and let the air out with a long, loud hisssssss.

Ernst the Eagle quickly turned and pointed to the hissing shrub. "M-m-m-monster," he whispered.

Cat tried to wave to get the Wizard's attention, but his arms were a little full.

Finally, the Wizard and Ronny the Robot made their way over to Cat.
"I heard a horrible hissing sound," said Ernst.
"I saw the shrub move," said Cat.
"Could be we have an uninvited guest," the Wizard began. "Like a garden snake, a gopher, or a giant snail perhaps."

The Wizard bravely tiptoed up to the shrub and slowly parted the leaves.

Standing there were Rosa and her Underworld friends.

"Surprise!" the Root Queen shouted gleefully.

"Aarghh!" Ernst cried as the Garden creatures scattered.

Viktor began to chomp on the bushes and flowers. "These are delicious!" he said.

The mummy took off for a game of Tag, but he tripped over his bandages. "Guess I'm 'it'!" he called.

The ghosts were trying to play a friendly game of 'Chase the Robot', but Cat sent Ronny hurrying away.

The Garden folk didn't understand that these creatures just wanted to play. But the Royal King and Queen understood. They were overjoyed to see their old friends. "Welcome!" the Queen said.

"No scary monsters at this celebration," said the King. "Just good friends."

"And friends who play together, stay together!" said Rosa.

Then the Wizard stepped up and shouted, "We've got games for everybody – monsters, creatures, Royals and Wizards!"

Suddenly, the garden birds and insects began to make music. The Funhouse friends started to shake, shimmy, twist and shout!

The Underworld creatures backed away and hid. They'd never seen anything like this before!

"Wh-wh-wh-what are you doing?" asked Mu.

"Why," said the Wizard, "we're dancing! Join us, it's fun!" Then he held his hand out to Rosa. "May I have this dance?"

Rosa was delighted!

Soon, everyone danced and played to their hearts' content. And the
Root Queen exclaimed, "What an abso-blooming-lutely perfect party!"

Printing: Litopat S.p.A., Italy 2016

We aim to provide as much inspiration as possible, but with minimal impact on the environment. All our books take the environment into account in every stage of production, from the choice of paper to how we distribute our printed material.

The book you are holding is printed on paper that meets all the requirements for responsible forestry. This means, for example, that the paper raw material comes from trees that are certified to originate from a sustainably managed forest. We print using vegetable-based printing inks without solvents, and the printers are located close to our large markets to avoid long-distance transport to you.

We are also working to develop the printed medium so that it minimises impact on the environment in the future. Read more about our environmental work at www.ikea.co.uk